www.somethingwickedlyweird.com

To read more about Stanley, look out for all the
Something Wickedly Weird books:

The Werewolf and the Ibis
The Ice Pirates
The Buccaneer's Bones
The Curse of the Wolf
The Smugglers' Secret
The Golden Labyrinth

Read more spooky tales in Dust 'n' Bones,
also by the award-winning Chris Mould.

And visit Chris at his website:
www.chrismouldink.com

THE BUCCANEER'S BONES

CHRIS MOULD

Hodder
Children's
Books

A division of Hachette Children's Books

For Ed Collier Jones

Text and illustrations copyright © 2007 Chris Mould

First published in Great Britain in 2007
by Hodder Children's Books
This paperback edition published 2010

2

A Catalogue record for this book is available from the British Library

ISBN 978 0 340 93104 2

Printed and bound in the UK by
CPI Bookmarque Ltd, Croydon, CR0 4TD

The paper and board used in this paperback by Hodder Children's Books
are natural recyclable products made from wood grown in sustainable
forests. The manufacturing processes conform to the environmental
regulations of the country of origin.

Hodder Children's Books
A division of Hachette Children's Books
338 Euston Road, London NW1 3BH
An Hachette UK company
www.hachette.co.uk

Admiral Swift

A The Wooden Mile
B The Lighthouse
C The Old Pirate Wreck
D Candlestick Hall
E The North Bay
F The Gypsy Camp
G Candlestick Cave
H The Harbour
I The Moor

Crampton Rock

the calm before the storm

Crampton Rock was still and silent. Early morning light spilled over the horizon on to the harbour. A flock of gulls hitched a ride on the gentle sea breeze and if you had been easily fooled you would have taken a good look and thought that this place was tranquil and serene. But despite the crispy blue sky and golden sands, all hell was about to break loose.

9

Something Wickedly Weird

*

Somewhere far away, a chill wind blew over an old buccaneers' graveyard that looked out over the coastline. A handful of crooked tombstones spilled across a grassy knoll.

The turf rippled and beneath it something clawed its way upward.

Pop.

The first of many hands scrabbled its way through the wormy black soil.

Then another. And another, until the festering remains of every grave were shifting silently.

Soon the ragged shapes of men were above ground, each before his own stone, blackened with clay and soil

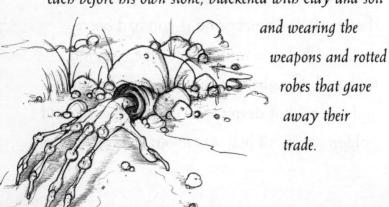 *and wearing the weapons and rotted robes that gave away their trade.*

'Summon the Devil's Horse,' croaked the first one. 'She is the best ship for the job.'

'Aye, aye, sir. So be it.' The man had a bullhorn over his shoulder on a length of rope. He raised it and blew his call. It sailed on the breeze and resounded across the water.

In a short while the filthy ship would appear, and they would set sail.

Gulls rested on the crowstepped roof of Candlestick Hall. Outside was the soothing view of Crampton Rock harbour, but an argument boiled within its walls.

11

Mrs Carelli, the housekeeper, had tracked down the new lord of the manor, young Stanley Buggles.

He was in serious trouble and she was hot on his heels.

'I cannot believe the scrapes and situations you have got me into since you inherited this old place, Stanley. We just go from one terrible mess to another. I don't know what your Great-Uncle Bart would have thought. He worked hard to shake off his pirate's reputation and live a normal life, and now it's all gone to pot. What will the ladies in the village think?'

'But—' began Stanley.

'We don't never have a moment's peace and every time I turn my back you've gotten us into more bunkum.'

'But Mrs Carelli, I—' Stanley tried.

'This little ol' fishing community lived in peace on this island before you turned up, Stanley. I'm too old for all this baloney.'

'Can I just say something ... I—'

'No, you can't. Your precious little Ibis has got us into more trouble than it's worth. All that trouble for a silver trinket.'

'It is not a *trinket*.' Stanley's voice was raised now and he was off. 'It has great power. If you ever hold it in your hands you will feel it, just like I did.'

'Stanley, listen. I want you to explain it to me again. It's not that I don't believe you, it's just that it's a little hard to take in,' said Mrs Carelli, holding the boy by his upper arms and staring deep into his eyes. 'Now, take it slowly.'

Stanley collected his thoughts and when he was ready he began.

'When I first came to Candlestick Hall I found the Ibis, nestled in the belly of the preserved pike in his glass case on the wall. The Ibis looked beautiful as I held her in my hands. There was no way I could have known, but in touching her I caused a tremor. It sent a shockwave that raised the first of an army of long-dead sea rogues and villains.'

'You know it sounds ridiculous,' muttered Mrs Carelli, 'but let's just say that's exactly what happened. What went wrong, Stanley? Where is the Ibis now?'

'She sits in the belly of the pike, who now swims in the lake out on the moor. The dear old pike knew the Ibis should not touch the water and that if she did, all the long-forgotten spirits of the evil pirate world would awaken. There is a name for it. It is what they call the quickening.

'But as we walked across the moor with him strapped across my back, I slipped and he ended up in the water. And now we sit in wait for the grim and the gruesome.'

'Stanley, it all sounds more than ridiculous, you must admit?' insisted Mrs Carelli.

'I know it does, but the pike has never lied to me or warned me of anything that didn't happen.'

'What on earth do you mean, lied to you?'

'Mrs Carelli, the pike speaks. In a strange tongue but nonetheless he very definitely speaks!' Stanley persisted.

'Well, that's the daftest load of old hog-wash I ever did hear. A talking pike! Well, he never said anything to me and I dusted him down a million times. The sooner you get ghostly pirates out o' your head, the better. I said you wasn't well and I know I'm right.

You need a good night's sleep, lad. And before you get any ideas, young man, I think your precious little Ibis is better off left where it is for now. Out o' sight and away from here.'

Stanley curled up his nose at the thought. He was determined to retrieve the pike and the Ibis as soon as possible.

There was a knock on the window. The top of a face appeared and a hand waved at them.

'That looks like Daisy from the lighthouse, Stanley,' sighed Mrs Carelli. 'Come in, poppet,' she shouted through the glass. 'Door's open.'

Daisy's fresh-faced entrance brought light into the room and poured ease on the argument.

'I brought fish from Uncle Lionel,' Daisy announced.

Stanley lifted the cloth on Daisy's

basket and as he did a live fish jumped into the air and slapped him on the face.

'Ouch!'

'Saves me doing it,' said Mrs Carelli as she wandered off into the kitchen.

One of the grim and grey shipmates pulled out a map. He pinned one corner of it to a wooden table with a nasty-looking blade hanging out of a shabby sleeve, and rolled out the rest with a grubby hand.

Another man stood behind him, peering over his shoulder at the greens and blues of the map. Taking a long knife from his inside pocket, he dropped it on a small olive-coloured shape in the south-westerly corner. It stuck in firmly, the blade swaying from side to side.

'That's where we wants to be, sir.'

'Fanking you kindly,' came a sneering reply. 'Best get goin', then. Hoist the mainsail, you dirty, stinkin' old sea dogs.'

While Stanley lay drifting in his bed that night, the creaking wooden shape of a rotting ship moved stealthily through the night. Its ragged black sails flapped violently in the wind and a band of grisly shipmates drank to their own good fortunes down below.

Soon there would be more. From far and wide they had begun to assemble, some in groups, some alone. All heading for the same corner of the earth.

2

Beyond the bronze Warrior

Stanley lay comfortably wrapped up in the warmth of his bed. He had drifted off into a deep sleep, with a candle still flickering by his bedside. The faint light picked his face out of the darkness until finally it petered out.

Stanley began to dream. In the dream he swam effortlessly through the lake out on the moor.

Deeper and deeper he went until there was nothing around him but a bottomless black.

Staring eyes and sharpened teeth soared up towards him from the abyss. It startled him before he realized it was his old friend the pike.

Circling about Stanley's head and drifting effortlessly around him, the pike began to speak.

'Help me, Stanley. It is time for me to return. Do not blame yourself for what happened to me; it was a mere accident. You are sitting in wait for the full force of the quickening to materialize and I fear that down here I cannot help you. Take me home, Stanley. The Ibis sits in my stomach and her heart beats so hard that it gives me the bellyache. I long for my place on the wall. I had grown to love my glass case, but I did not realize until I was without it. I fear I am growing old, and though at one time the cold did not bother me, now it bites at my bones and I long for the warmth of the house.'

Suddenly Stanley felt the urge to reach the surface. He soared quickly upwards, desperate to grab a breath of air. As he burst through, it woke him with a start.

He sat up wide-eyed in his bed, peering into the gloom.

'Just a dream,' he said, lying back down.

But the dream would not leave him alone. It repeated itself all night and woke him endlessly, until the morning light pierced through the tiny hole in the heavy curtains.

A rotted flag waved through the mist. Grim voices bellowed through the darkness.

A crash of waves broke across the quarterdeck and drenched the ghastly crew.

Down in the cabin, three poisoned-looking faces sat together at a large wooden table, spilling grog across the maps.

A rogue tattooed from head to toe raised his tankard.

'I swear that as long as my rotten spirit wanders

this earth, I, Scribbles Flanaghan, will seek out the Ibis and bring it 'ome to its rightful place, 'ere on board the **Rusty Blade**. And if we 'appen to spy the silver casket on our travels, well, that is ours also. Do you swear by the same, Mister Smiff?' he asked his nearest partner.

'That I do, Mister Scribbles, sir. That I do,' said Seafood Smith. He popped another crab claw open and swallowed it down with a swig of ale.

'And what about yerself there, Mister Doyle? Will yer be saying the same?'

'You can count on Doyle, me hearties. I will fight to the end to take back what once was mine.' He pulled a pair of nasty-looking pliers from his top pocket. 'I always 'as a little trick up me sleeve to get what I want. They don't call me Doyle the Dentist for nothin',' he sneered as he opened and closed his pincers. They all laughed out loud.

Someone rattled down the staircase from up on deck, spluttering and gasping and soaked in sea wash.

'Mister Scribbles, sir, permission to speak, sir.'

'Out with it, Mister Phipps. What is troubling you?'

'There's another ship, sir. A pirate ship, sir, up ahead. She looks like getting there afore us.'

'Well get a move on then, Phipps, and stop blubberin'.' Scribbles raised his voice and sent a grog bottle hurtling at the back of Phipps' head. 'The Rusty Blade will not be beaten by any other ship.'

Stanley had drifted off again. He was rudely
awakened by the sound of someone rapping at
the front door.

He listened out for Mrs Carelli and sure
enough her footsteps clomped across the
polished floor of the hallway.

'Hello, poppet,' he heard her say. He knew
it was Daisy – Mrs Carelli used that name for
her and for nobody else.

In the short time that Stanley had known
Daisy they had become firm friends, and
already they had been through thick and thin
together. It was a short walk from her uncle's
lighthouse to the Hall and she spent much of
her time at Stanley's side.

Stanley gathered himself together and
thundered down the staircase, desperate to
tell Daisy about his dream. But only when
Mrs Carelli was out of the way.

He waited for his moment and then he pounced. It was strange to retell the story in daylight.

'But it's only a dream, Stanley,' reassured Daisy. 'It doesn't really mean anything.'

'Daisy, listen. We can't leave the Ibis where it is. It is vulnerable, and if we have it we can protect it. If we leave it in the water, they will come and take it easily without any challenge. The dream is a warning. We must act.'

'All right, then. When?'

'Soon. But when we return with the pike we must hide him. Mrs Carelli won't be happy if she knows that he is back here, with the Ibis in his belly. We need a hiding place, somewhere that doesn't get cleaned regularly. But that rules out the whole of the house!'

'It is time for me to show you something,' announced Daisy. 'I haven't got round to telling you about this, but now the time is right.'

Stanley narrowed his eyes at her. 'The time is right for what?'

Daisy took him by the hand and led him through the winding corridors of the ground floor of the house, past the maze of pictures encased in huge wooden frames and strange objects in cabinets.

Stanley was intrigued. Even now, Daisy still knew the old place better than he did. When she used to clean for Mrs Carelli she had been in every nook and cranny there was to find.

Finally they stood at the end of a corridor, facing the figure of an ancient warrior cast in bronze.

'What do you think, Stanley?'

'What do I think? Well, yes, it's very impressive but ... I've seen it before. I've been here long enough to know it was there. Daisy, what has this got to do with anything?'

She giggled to herself. 'You really have no idea, do you?'

The figure held a broadsword in its hand. Daisy gripped the sword's handle and pulled, making a satisfying *clunk*. Then she grabbed the front of the figure and heaved at it.

It suddenly became obvious to Stanley that it worked as a huge door.

'Help me, then!' Daisy requested.

Stanley was mesmerized and didn't move for a moment.

'It's amazing what you find by accident when you're dusting,' Daisy said as Stanley gathered himself together and helped her to pull the heavy casing wide open. A blast of cold air rushed out at him from inside. He couldn't see what was up ahead, but it appeared to be some kind of tunnel.

'Where does it go?' he asked, grinning
from ear to ear.

'Why don't you find
out?' said Daisy, smiling. 'You'll need
a light.'

Stanley ran to his room and returned,
clattering down the steps, with the small
candleholder that had been perched by
his bed.

'What you up to, young Buggles?' came
a voice.

'Nothing, Mrs Carelli, I promise.' And he

disappeared too quickly to be interrogated.

In a moment Stanley was winding his way into the darkness with Daisy clutching on to his shoulder. The way ahead was black and narrow.

Their heads were near the roof of the tunnel, and they had to bend slightly to save themselves from taking a bump.

The passage seemed to be never-ending, turning and twisting. All the while Daisy hung on behind Stanley and urged him onward.

Just when Stanley thought it would never stop, the path began to open out.

He thought he could hear the rush of the sea in the distance. 'Go on,' Daisy said. 'You're nearly there.'

Shortly, they were standing in a huge cave where the sea came in to form a large pool. A circular opening led out to where the water crashed against the rocks on the south side of the island. Bits of driftwood swam in the foamy water that spilled over the limestone. All around them were craggy platforms and hiding places. An old cupboard lay lopsided against a wall of rock, and a little wooden rowing boat was tied to a stone pillar.

'I love it!' cried Stanley as he turned to Daisy. She could hardly hear him. The wind whistled through the cave's opening and the crash of the surf almost drowned out his voice.

'Why the cupboard?' he asked.

Daisy shrugged her shoulders and held her hands aloft. 'Don't know!'

'Why didn't you tell me before?' he shouted through the thunder of the water.

'Well, I've hardly had the time,' she answered. 'We've both been more than busy since we met!' She came closer so that she could be heard more easily. 'Stanley, we should get back. Mrs Carelli will be suspicious.'

'Does she know about this place?'

'No, but she will if we don't get a move on. We can return when we need to. Come on!'

Stanley looked at his candle. The gust had wiped out its flame.

'Prepare yourself, Daisy,' he announced. 'We'll have to make our way in the dark.'

And she held on to the tail of his waist-coat as they felt their way back through the blinding blackness.

3

Out from the Tomb

An ancient stone block began to shift and disturbed the stalks and tendrils that had held it fast for a thousand years. Hordes of spiny black insects were startled into movement in every direction.

A skeletal hand with brittle, blackened nails curled itself around the crumbling slab and forced a meagre gap.

Two narrowed eyes peered out from the black pit.

35

And then, snake-like, the bony frame of Angel Cuzco slithered out from his prison. Dressed in red, he had a shock of white hair, with stumps upon his back.

Nearby, an identical stone moved sideways and out climbed two more figures. They were dreadful in every way, swathed in long coats embedded with silt and sand, stinking and soggy. Long, lank hair hung over their clavicles and their red bloodshot eyes struggled in the light that they had not seen for so many years.

'What names do you go by?' asked Angel Cuzco.

'I am Captain Alvaro Villegas and this is my twin brother, Mauricio,' said one of the siblings.

'I remember you. We fought together along the coast of South America,' claimed the Angel as he felt his rusty memory come back to life. 'We were the pride of Peru for many years. Everyone feared us. You, Alvaro, were my captain and we were, all of us, like a band of brothers.'

The twins stared, their memories coming back too. They remembered the might of Angel Cuzco and how they had been proud to fight for each other like mad dogs.

'Why did you waken from your ancient tombs?' asked the Angel.

'The same reason that you did,' declared Alvaro. 'The Ibis is alive, and the silver casket sits in wait for the final piece in the jigsaw. Will you join us on the journey from Peru?'

A green glow appeared in the Angel's eyes, a fire from within. His passion for the Ibis was strong. Stronger than anybody's, he thought.

'No. I shall not join you. I shall go alone, and when I reach the home of the Ibis I will take it for myself and no one and nothing will stop me.'

He said no more. And before they could show their surprise he had drawn his sword and cut them in two.

Their bodies lay slumped at his feet. He grinned the most evil grin, which turned into vicious laughter. It rang out into the air, causing the parrots to flock away from the branches above.

He pulled back the lid of the ancient tomb and threw

the brothers' filthy bones back inside.

Only then did he set off. He walked for days until he reached Arequipa and then headed to the southern coast. When at last he reached the sea, he kept on walking. There was no boat or ship to take him, and nor did he care. He simply kept on going in the right direction. The water washed around his feet and he felt his weight sink slightly into the sand. Shoals of sea life darted around him.

Soon his submerged body was walking along the sea bed. His lank hair floated at the back of him with his coat tails, his sword was drawn at his side.

On he went through night and day, through light and dark. As he walked he spoke these words:

'Drive my ancient spirit unto the sacred bird. Deliver thy casket forged of silver. Prepare for the coming of the Angel, for he walks alone among the dead.'

If he had said it a million times he would surely say it a million times more. Over and over it went.

Small bones and fossils were crushed beneath his feet as he trod along the cloudy sea bed. His blade swished through the water and on he marched, deeper and deeper into the sea.

In search of
the Ibis

Stanley and Daisy were busy discussing the
Ibis. It was time to get their hands on it,
whether Mrs Carelli liked the idea or not.
Perhaps she would be too busy cleaning to
notice what they were up to.

'What's the plan then,
Stanley?' asked Daisy
cheerfully.

'The plan, Daisy, is that we don't have a plan,' he announced.

'Very well,' she sighed, and they set off together over the moor.

The wind was against them and it was harsh out on the hills. There were not many days when you wouldn't feel the worst of the weather there, in one of its many forms.

They passed the old water mill and Stanley remembered the harsh winter, when they had ventured out together into the blinding snow.

It wasn't long before they were back at the lake. It was calm and serene, save for the wind blowing ripples across the surface and the reeds shaking in the breeze.

Stanley and Daisy stood staring across the water for some time. They did not really know what they should do about retrieving the pike, but it was peaceful and right now they were happy to sit and enjoy the moment.

Soon the wind dropped and the sun broke out. It was cold, but now the water had become completely still.

'We should have brought a picnic, Stanley,' laughed Daisy.

'Yes, what a shame that we are empty-handed,' said Stanley.

But at that moment the huge body of the pike speared out from the water and landed neatly in his arms. Freezing water drenched Stanley from head to foot and the icy body of the fish chilled him through.

The pike wriggled himself into comfort and began to speak.

'Ahh, Stanley. I knew in my heart that you would have the good sense to return. Now let us take to the hills and we can get me home, where the warmth of the Hall awaits me. I have had quite enough of the dark depths of the lake. I don't think I shall be returning, not just yet!'

Stanley and Daisy looked at one another with raised eyebrows.

'Come along, come along. I will catch cold out here in the open air,' instructed the pike. 'Once you put me in place, we can discuss your next move. There is much to be done.'

'Do you still have the Ibis?' questioned Stanley.

'My dear boy, of course I do. Why do you underestimate me so?'

'I wasn't sure if I could trust you once you'd entered the water!' Stanley admitted.

'Well in all my watery days, I have never been so insulted,' the pike started – and as the unlikely trio marched across the moor, the argument continued.

They weren't sure how to approach the house safely, and decided that they would slip in through the fuel store at the back of the house and into the kitchen. From there they would sneak across the ground floor and wind their way unseen through the maze of corridors to where the bronze warrior stood in wait for them.

Gingerly, they crept towards the garden gate, taking a good look at the back of the house. All was quiet. Or so they thought.

Unbeknown to them, Mrs Carelli was pottering by a bedroom window which looked out over the garden.

Something caught her eye out on the moor. She looked up: nothing. Must have been a bird.

As she moved to the back of the room, doing this and that, Stanley and Daisy hoiked the pike across the lawn.

Mrs Carelli moved back to dust the window. She could hear noises, but by then Stanley and Daisy had clambered through the opening to the fuel store.

'Strange,' said Mrs Carelli to herself. 'Young Buggles is up to something, I swear it.'

She pressed her face to the window and peered down. But as she questioned the whereabouts of Stanley, the three were already out of the kitchen and winding their way carefully through the corridors towards the bronze warrior.

Their feet raced across the floor, and at last Stanley and Daisy reached the lonesome soldier.

Daisy tugged at the handle. It was stuck!

The familiar clang of Mrs Carelli's brass dustpan resounded nearby. They looked up in panic. She wasn't there, but she was close.

'Hurry, Daisy, hurry!' pleaded Stanley.

'I'm trying,' she panicked.

And then the pike started. 'Stanley, where is this? I did not request to be placed in this part of the house.'

'Quiet!' insisted Stanley.

'Is that you, Master Buggles?' came a familiar voice.

CLUNK. Daisy had done it. But she was forced to pull the heavy door open by herself as Stanley stood with his arms full, frustrated.

After a few seconds that felt like as many minutes, the gap was forced wide enough for them to sneak through. Once inside, they pulled it shut, realizing that they were without a light to show the way. Daisy braved going first, and pulled Stanley along as his arms were occupied.

'Ridiculous,' continued the pike. 'It is as cold and dark in here as in the dreary lake. This is a punishment, is it not?'

They felt their way through the darkness.

'Where will we put him?' quizzed Daisy.

'What about the old cupboard?' suggested Stanley.

'Yes. Good,' said Daisy.

When they finally reached it, Stanley was desperate to be rid of the weight. He hurled the pike through the door and it landed with a thud.

'This is nothing short of abuse and bullying!' persisted the pike. 'I was not aware I would lose my status in the house simply because I've been away a short while. How can I be an adviser from here? Ridiculous!'

After waves of protest they finally closed the door on the ill-tempered pike, but his voice resounded through the casing of the cupboard. What if it echoed through the cave and was heard in the house?

Stanley gritted his teeth. 'Please bear with us. We cannot let Mrs Carelli know we've rescued you. It's either here or the lake, I'm afraid.'

Stanley knew that would shut him up and sure enough, the pike was absolutely silent. Stanley had great respect for the pike, but there were times when he had all the qualities of a badly behaved dog.

They closed the bronze door on the dear old pike and headed back into the hallway.

'That's that sorted then,' smiled Stanley, turning to Daisy, who was staring over his shoulder. Mrs Carelli was standing behind him, peering at the two of them with one raised eyebrow.

'That's *what* sorted?' she asked. 'You're up to something, Stanley. Something sinister. I do hope it's not one o' your crazy plans.'

The Legend of Angel Cuzco

Much later, Stanley was in his favourite room, which was full of drawers with interesting contents. He searched through the piles of books and papers. Could he find something to stop the coming of the ghostly villains who were headed their way? Was there anything he and Daisy could say or do that would be of assistance?

He had searched all afternoon and not
found much, but one scrappy piece of old
parchment caught his attention. It was a
letter. The top part was missing, but beneath
it was clear.

An icy chill trickled through Stanley as he
read it and he decided he needed to find
Daisy. It was something to be shared.

Stanley ran down the stairs shouting
Daisy's name. She was in the scullery, leafing
through a book.

A steaming kettle stood on the hearth.
Seats were huddled around the warmth of
the fireplace and Stanley sat down at Daisy's
side, placing himself in a tall wing-backed
chair.

'The first part is missing, Daisy, but listen
to this.'

*Do you know who comes to find you?
Have you seen their deadly figures, their
ragged bones and stinking foul faces? They
belong to nightmares. To tales of woe and
terror.*

*Do you know of the legend of Angel
Cuzco?*

Stanley stopped, and he and Daisy looked
at one another. The two of them huddled
together around the fire and Stanley
continued.

*The Angel was the scourge of the South
American coast. Often he joined forces with
others, but he was known to like his own
company and he feared no one. Dressed in
scarlet, with plaited golden-white hair and
nut-brown skin, he was a sight to be sure.*

Something Wickedly Weird

It was maybe two hundred years ago that the Ibis sat buried in a church in Cuzco. It rested under a stone slab of a tomb adorned with the statue of an angel.

They say the power of the Ibis was so strong that the body returned to life in the form of the angel and stole away with the sacred bird. In a bid to keep it, the angel wore the robes of the pirate trade and fled to the east.

He fought so hard to keep it that he became the most feared buccaneer of the seven seas.

He lost the Ibis when he was overcome by a ship of monstrous buccaneers.

It is said that his evil ways reduced his wings to stumps upon his back and that in the end he died defending a gang of Peruvian brothers that he had befriended.

If I were you, I would gather my belongings and escape while there is still a chance that I shall see you again.

Make haste.

Your affectionate brother,

And the rest was torn away.

'Is that a true story, Stanley?' asked Daisy who, despite the roaring fire, was shaking like a leaf.

'Well, maybe it is and maybe it isn't. But I'm sure that sooner or later, we will be finding out.' Stanley folded it back into its age-old creases and returned it to its drawer.

The Timber Trail

That night, Stanley and Daisy looked out to the
darkness of the ocean from the staircase window.
A huge boat had arrived in the harbour.

'They're here,' panicked Stanley. The pair of
them peered more intently through the glass,
squinting their eyes.

'That's no pirate ship, Stanley. It's a ferry!'
claimed Daisy.

Voices could be heard from on board, shouts and laughter. The two of them stood watching, not knowing what was ahead.

Then there was movement. Something began to move down the gangplanks at one end of the boat. The fire baskets were burning, and they illuminated a long winding shape that snaked upward into the harbour, moving towards the moor. It was creaking and grinding like the train that had brought Stanley to the island. What was it?

Stanley and Daisy looked more closely still, and soon they realized that what was coming toward them was a trail of wooden wagons,

one behind another. Flickering lamps hung
from them, dancing in the dark. Song and
laughter bellowed from within.

They ran from room to room, chasing the
trail from window to window.

'Travellers,' said Daisy. 'They are travellers,
and they have been here before. Good
people they are, with many friends on
Crampton Rock. They will be welcomed.
They pitch up on the moor when they are
here, but recently the curse of the werewolf
had driven them away,

because many were lost in its grip. They
must know the beast is gone – they say that
word travels fast in the world of the
travelling man.'

On they went to the moor, and when they
were far enough out they rested in a large
circle. The light from a campfire laid an
orange cast across the hill and the howl of
dogs sailed eerily through the night air. A
tent was pitched and sat comfortably
protected by the wagons. Silhouettes of
people moved around in the warm glow.

The fire danced all night and Stanley
fell asleep to the distant sounds of laughing
and singing.

In the morning he was sitting with a warm
drink by the fire when a knock at the door
disturbed the moment. A tall gypsy man

stood in the early light.
He had long hair and
wore clogs. A heavy
coat hung from his
shoulders, tied with
rope around the waist.
He unfastened it.

'I come to thank
the good lady for
the fresh water
when we arrived,'
he chirped. He had
an accent that was
strange to Stanley,
and his manner was
pleasant. He pulled his
coat open to show a brace
of rabbits, and handed
them to Stanley.

'Oh … erm, thank you!' said Stanley.

'You must be the lad,' the man added. 'I wanted to see you.'

'Oh! About what?' Stanley quizzed.

'You misunderstand me, son,' he said. 'I mean, I wanted to see what you looked like.'

Stanley looked confused. Daisy joined him at the door and they glanced at each other with raised eyebrows.

'The name's Phinn. The folks would like to see you,' the man said, confusing Stanley further. 'So when you're ready, come along.'

And he clomped down the path in his clogged feet and walked back across the moor.

Mrs Carelli was behind Stanley now. She placed warm hands across his shoulders.

'Don't worry, Stanley. They are good people. They were the first ones on the

island, and they gave this place to us.
Sometimes they are here for months, and
sometimes only days. But this time they come
for you. Among other things they
bring help and they bring
hope. We may
have a fight on
our hands, but
all is not lost.
Not yet.'

They looked
out to sea and
wondered what would
show itself next over the horizon.

'The pirates are coming,' said Stanley. 'And
we cannot keep them at bay for ever.'

'Go and see the travellers, Stanley. They
may hold the answer to our problems,'
suggested Mrs Carelli.

Stanley went to get himself ready. In half an hour he would be climbing up on to the moor.

7

the Glass Ball

'Will you come with me, Daisy?' asked
Stanley, wrapping his coat around him.

'Of course,' she replied, and they made
their way out of the kitchen door and
across the back lawn to the rusted gate.
They trod the beaten track on to the moor
where the home of the travellers waited
for them.

As they drew near they could see that
there were more tents pitched around the
central one and that the fire was still burning.
Small children ran in
and out of the
wagons and

lank dogs with missing legs meandered
aimlessly around the camp.

Stanley remembered his first encounters
with the dogs of Crampton Rock: all of them
with lost limbs, and all of them escaped
victims of the werewolf. Here was a sure sign
that the travellers were no strangers to
this peculiar island.

A group of people were standing around in a ring, and in the middle two giant men were boxing each other bravely with bare hands.

It was strange to see so much activity out on the moor.

But when Stanley and Daisy came close, everything stopped. People turned and looked, putting down their tools or whatever they were holding. The children stopped playing and the boxers lowered their fists.

They all came forward and held out their hands to Stanley. Shortly, Phinn appeared again. He stood on a cartwheel and addressed everyone.

'This young man is Stanley Buggles. He banished the curse of the wolf from these lands, killing the beast that took our brothers and leaving us free to settle here whenever we please.'

The crowd cheered and the people shook Stanley's hand and ruffled his hair. One of the boxers picked him up and carried him above his head. They arrived at one of the tents and Phinn followed, bringing Daisy with him.

The boxer placed Stanley back on his feet and held out a giant hand. 'My name is Bartley. My brother was taken from me by the wolf, and I wear his memory on my heart. Thank you, boy,' he said. 'I will be forever grateful to you.'

He had the biggest, strongest hands that Stanley had ever seen, yet he seemed as gentle as it was possible to imagine.

Inside the tent, an old woman sat at a small table. A length of fabric was thrown over it, concealing the legs and lower section. On top there was an object covered in a velvet cloth. Two halves of a barrel were placed at her side to form a pair of seats.

She invited the guests to sit down and be comfortable, and someone brought a strange drink that boiled with smoke. They didn't dare ask what was in it, but they drank it and licked their lips and asked for more.

'My name is Greta,' said the old woman. She had a soft, gentle voice and she was craggy with skin of a warm brown colour. 'We want to help you, Stanley. You are a friend of the gypsies now, and your enemies are ours also. Give me your hands.'

Stanley held them out to her and she clutched them in her own. They were dry and creased, but smooth to touch and warmer than his. Then she took the velvet sheet away and revealed a glass ball in the middle of the table.

'Lay them on the crystal. It will help,' she said, staring hard into the sphere. 'Do you see them, Stanley? Do you see what awaits you?'

It meant nothing to Stanley. He could not see anything except for the glass ball with his hands on the top and the old woman gazing into it with her face lighting up in surprise.

'What ... what is it?' asked Stanley.

'They come from all corners of the earth. And they come in their thousands. From the depths of the ground they stir, like swarms of poisonous insects. Of all the enemies that come, one ship sails alone. When she arrives she will settle in the north bay. She wears the Yellow Jack and none will come near her.'

'What does that mean?' piped up Daisy.

'The Yellow Jack is the flag flown in warning of the fever,' Greta explained.

'You mean that one of the ships is filled with pirates who are ill?'

'Yes, dreadfully ill. They have the *buccaneer's bones*, a disease to punish the worst of any pirate spirits. But they will try and get here all the same. The Ibis draws them near.'

'We must be extra careful to avoid the sickness then,' said Stanley.

'It cannot harm you, Stanley. It is an illness of those who wander the earth in their skeletal form. The spirit is willing, but the body turns putrid and poisonous and burns itself out through a ghastly fever. Foul and stinking is the stench of buccaneer's bones.

You will surely know it if you come across it.'

'And what of the Ibis? How did you know of it, and that it's here?' asked Stanley.

'The legend is older than all of us. The sacred bird has been to more places than all the travellers here put together, and lived a million lifetimes. Most people know nothing of it and of the ones that do, some are good, some bad. Many think they own it, but very few deserve it.

'Your image came to me in my crystal ball when you defeated the wolf. I watched you out there on the moor, brave and alone. From then on your shape showed itself many times in the crystal and I saw you through the spiralling fog of the glass when you discovered the Ibis.

'Right now what matters is that those villains know the Ibis is here, and they want it.

There are many travelling men here, Stanley, tough, hard men who will fight to protect you. But they are up against it.

'Strong is he who fights by the side of his own brother. But unbeatable is the man who walks in the shadow of his own death.'

Greta looked into the ball again, her face nearing the glass.

'Who is this who walks along the ocean floor, dressed in red with a shock of white hair and a cutting blade held at his side? With eyes of green, and stumps upon his back?'

Stanley and Daisy froze. They knew right there and then that Angel Cuzco was more than just a legend.

Greta watched carefully. In the murky darkened depths, weary pirate bones were assembling back together out of their old sea chest. A pair of skeletal companions dressed their ragged selves, their rusted weapons hanging from their hands. A broken padlock lay at their feet and the chest was scattered in splinters upon the murky sand.

But two green eyes shone in the bubbling blue, and with blinding speed the Angel was marching upon them. He cut them through without pausing and sent their limbs floating like dead fish until they settled in the sand.

'Enough,' Greta said. She knew that what she had seen disturbed Stanley and Daisy, and that if she told them any more she would only frighten them further.

The Black Swarm

In the days that followed, Stanley found
himself spending more time with his new-
found friends. Bartley watched him shadow-
box and showed him tricks and techniques as
they sparred playfully. The big man would
hold out his hands as Stanley hooked and
jabbed into his palms.

'You have a good pair of hands, Stanley.

Quick and precise. But I warn you, you may need them sooner than you think.'

'I know,' said Stanley, 'and I will be ready.' But he knew in his heart of hearts that no man on earth was strong enough to defeat the evil spirits of the dead, and he was plotting a way to keep the island safe from the deadly crew that moved towards them.

Meanwhile, Daisy was making herself popular bringing fresh fish to the camp.

'Courtesy of Mister Grouse, from the lighthouse,' she would say, handing over a box of sea bream or mackerel. Then she'd hang around all day, playing with the dogs and the children, until Stanley had tired of his training with the mighty Bartley.

Two more days had passed and Stanley knew that what was coming in their direction

would arrive sooner or later. He knew
nothing of how far the pirates had travelled,
how long they would take or which way
they would come. But still he knew for sure
that eventually they would appear, and his
anxiety grew and grew until it turned his
stomach into a twisting, knotted pain.

The very next morning was bleak and
black. It was almost as if the sun had not
woken, and a misty fog circled the harbour
all day. It might well have been the weather,
but the whole mood of the island
seemed to turn,

almost as if it knew what was coming.

Black clouds hung heavily over the sea, rolling and rumbling in a brisk wind.

Then, as night was arriving, something poked through the tops of the misty clouds in the far distance. At first it appeared like a flock of crows, flapping on the wind. But no. It moved too slowly and steadily.

'Flags,' said Stanley. 'They are black pirate flags.' And as he said it he knew he was right, and his heart sank into his belly. 'There is only one thing to do, Daisy,' he said calmly.

'And what is that?' said Daisy, staring into his face. 'Aren't you terrified?'

'No, Daisy, I am not. I am *prepared*. At nightfall, I will take the Ibis and be gone. You must cover for me. The ships are close again and I must act soon.'

'Let me come with you,' she begged.

'No way.'

'What makes you think you can handle this more than me?' she said angrily, tucking a playful punch into his belly.

'Ooof. All right,' he answered, granting her wish. 'If you want to be part of it you can. But it will be the hardest thing you ever did.'

And that was that. In that instant it was decided.

Within five minutes they were feeling their way through the blackness of the tunnel.

When he reached the cupboard, Stanley
grabbed the pike hurriedly.

'Dear oh dear, whatever next,' began
the pike. 'I was just beginning to grow
comfortable.'

Daisy climbed into the little wooden boat
as Stanley handed her the pike and pushed
them away from the rocks. When he was
soaking wet up to his waist, he jumped in.

'Hold on tight to your slippery friend
there, Daisy. We don't want him to end up in
the drink!' warned Stanley.

'I am sure you are fully aware that I am a
freshwater creature,'
muttered the pike.
'I am far too
sophisticated
to dwell among
the dregs of marine life.'

'You would get on well with my mother,'
said Stanley. 'It's just a shame you will never
make her acquaintance.' He began to row
with all his might, pushing them out through
the narrow opening on to the ocean surf.
They were round the other side of the island
now, away from the onslaught of piracy.

A full moon was pouring light across the
harbour, and the mischievous pair readied
themselves in their trusty boat. But Stanley
soon found he was no oarsman. He couldn't
control the boat, no matter how he tried.

'You take hold of our friend here,' said
Daisy, 'and I'll do the rowing. I don't think
you've found your sea legs yet,' she joked.

She took the oars from him and
immediately the ride became sure and
steady. Stanley watched her rowing:
despite the rough water, she made it

seem effortless. And for someone quite small she was surprisingly strong.

'Where are we heading?' asked Daisy.

'To the north side of the island,' said Stanley. 'To where the Yellow Jack is heading with its sickly crew.'

'Stanley, what on earth are you thinking of? We are supposed to be avoiding them, not joining them!' Daisy panicked. Suddenly the boat was carried along on the crest of a wave,

and Daisy fought hard to keep them from
crashing against the rocks.

'Trust me, Stanley,' she panted, pulling
harder on the oars as the little boat bobbed
up and down on the swell.

Then as they cleared the rocks and came
out into the deep, they saw
ships heading towards
them from the other
direction.

'Row, Daisy!'
cried Stanley.
'Row for your
life!'

'I'm trying,'
she gasped, as
the drag of the
water yanked at
her arms.

Stanley had not planned on a choppy sea. The harbour had seemed relatively calm but here on the other side of the island they were struggling to steady the boat. White froth rushed up the sides and the splashes of water were icy cold.

Before too long, the shape of Crampton Rock was growing smaller as they steered away from the island and the pirate ships.

Darkness and endless water surrounded the little boat. On board, the two warriors headed fearlessly into the unknown.

Stanley announced to the pike something that he knew would not be popular.

'I'm going to take the Ibis from you,' he said.

'I had a feeling this was coming, and I fear that you are making a wrong move, Stanley,' the pike returned. 'I think perhaps there is a better way.'

'I don't think you have a better way,' said Stanley. 'Firstly, you have no idea what my plan is and secondly, if you do and there is an easier solution I'd like to know what it is.'

'I'm thinking!' insisted the pike, and he closed his mouth tightly so that Stanley had no chance of retrieving the Ibis.

'This is no time for games,' came Stanley, who felt a growing frustration. 'Open wide, please.'

But the mouth stayed shut and the eyes glared at him.

'Very well,' said Stanley, thinking quickly. 'If you refuse to cooperate, then I shall have no option but to place you in the salt water among the sea life.'

'Mmmm. I hear the tiger sharks are particularly hungry at this time of year,' suggested Daisy. She still wasn't entirely sure of Stanley's plan but nonetheless she was prepared to see it through.

The pike's eyes seemed to stare even wider as Stanley lifted him up and dangled him by his tail. The Ibis rolled to the front of his mouth and finally he allowed it to drop into the bottom of the boat.

'Thank you,' said Stanley. He didn't want to upset the pike, but time was of the essence. He retrieved the Ibis from the boat and slipped it neatly inside a square of cloth.

They rounded a cliff face, and suddenly a blackened shape hung over them. A filthy silhouette of sheer evil swayed on the surf. Voices bellowed out, and the torn and ragged shapes of sails flapped noisily in the gust.

Stanley and Daisy were dwarfed by the might of its hulking shape and they huddled tightly beneath it. On board, lamplights twinkled like stars here and there. The ship's name was painted on its side. The *Rusty Blade*.

Daisy had to steer right up to the under-side of the ship. It wasn't easy, by any means, but somehow she managed it.

'Perfect,' said Stanley. 'Hang on here.' He pulled himself up on to the side of the boat with the aid of the anchor chain that speared downward through the water. He had the Ibis tucked neatly into his inside pocket.

There was no one on deck. That was a stroke of luck. Stanley crept across the boards to the main mast and clambered up towards the yellow flag. Then when he could grasp hold of it, he tore it hastily from the ropes and shoved it inside his shirt.

'*Now* where on earth are
you going?' whispered Daisy
as loud as she dared.

'Just making a little
delivery,' Stanley said,
waving the Ibis at her
with a spare hand.

Daisy was confused,
but she trusted his
judgement and
knew that if she
did her job
and kept
the boat
right there
waiting for
him, everything
would be all
right.

She sat and watched him lurch down the barnacled side of the rotting ship. He wasn't far from the water before he stopped and dug his hand into a rotted hole. He tore at it fiercely until it was big enough for him to sneak through. Bits of splintered wood plopped into the waves.

Daisy cringed, clenching her sweating hands into fists. She did not know what she would do if someone appeared. She watched until the soles of Stanley's shoes were the last thing to drop through the hole.

Inside, Stanley crept around in the dark. He had stumbled into the crew's quarters, and knew that he had to scramble his way down to the stores at the bottom of the ship without being found by any of the spirits that lurked on board.

He felt his way along the slime and grease

that seemed to cake the ship's sides. Voices grew nearer. Too near.

Stanley hurried as much as he could. He had decided to place the Ibis in the ballast at the bottom of the ship. Here it would be concealed, and no one would stumble on it. And he could return and reclaim it after all this was over. Simple! he thought.

Something opened up to reveal a lower level. He stepped down carefully and felt for the floor beneath him. A layer of cold hard stones. This was it, the ballast. The stones were used as a weight to stabilize the frame of the ship.

In the far corner, he found a memorable spot. Bilge rats scurried over his hands and round his feet as he buried his fingers through the hard rugged surface that cut at his knuckles. He buried the Ibis right there, wrapped in its cloth protection.

And then he made his way through the
blackness the way he had come.

'What's that?' asked Scribbles Flanaghan,
pricking up an ear,
and his dreadful
figure stepped
into the light of
the oil lamp.
A cascade
of
endless tattoos
were illuminated
in the dark and his
two yellowy eyes
opened wider.

'I can 'ear somethin'.
Down in the stores. Ain't
no one down in the stores,

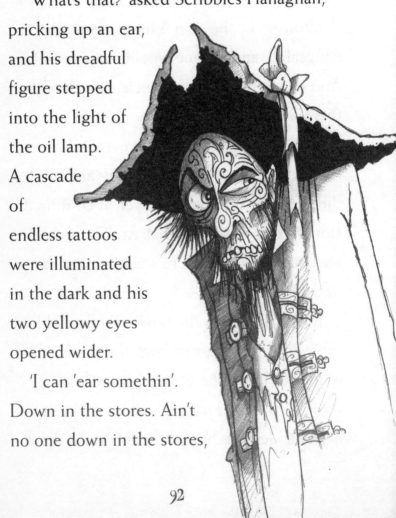

is there? Mister Smiff, will you be so kind as to investigate and while you're at it, take Mister Doyle with yer in case someone needs a reminder that we ain't 'ere to be messed with!'

'Aye, aye, Mister Flanaghan, sir. Seafood Smiff at your service.' He got to his feet, swallowing a handful of cockles, and was followed by Doyle into the damp darkness of the hold.

Stanley was still feeling his way back and he cringed as he creaked on the floorboards.

'There's someone 'ere, or that's a huge rat I can 'ear,' said Doyle. 'And when I get my 'ands on 'em I'm gonna do 'em some damage.'

Abruptly and unintentionally, Stanley's out-stretched hand landed in Doyle's grisly face.

'Agghhhh!' They both screamed, but Doyle held on to Stanley's arm and twisted it as he gripped.

'Who goes there? Friend or foe?' said
Doyle as he squeezed tightly.
Stanley felt the cold slimy grip of death.
Whatever or whoever

it was that held him stunk to high heaven. He held his free hand over his mouth.

'Nothing ... nobody ... I mean ...' struggled Stanley as he tried to think of the right thing to say. Doyle's gruesome face came closer through the dark. He was holding up a pair of pliers.

'Over 'ere, Mister Smiff,' grumbled Doyle to his companion. 'We got a customer for the dentist's chair.'

Stanley *really* didn't like the sound of that.

The foul-smelling twosome leered at him through the dim light. Their yellowy eyes came far too close.

'It's a boy! An ugly little feller 'e is an' all,' claimed Doyle. 'Shall we kill 'im now?'

'O' course we will,' Smith croaked. 'We'll do it with this.' He shoved a cutlass under Stanley's nose.

Stanley panicked. But he was now only an arm's length from the hole where he had squeezed in. He lunged for the escape route with his free hand and began pulling himself out.

Doyle held on to him tightly, but his arm was forced through the hole along with Stanley.

Smith lunged at him through the dark, swinging his blade, but he just kept hacking at the side of the ship. Chips and splinters of rotten wood fell to the floor as he swore in frustration.

Daisy looked up at Stanley in panic; she could see he was in trouble. But before she could act, he was out. He had shoved the weight of his body through the hole, and now he was dropping headlong into the boat. Daisy let out a piercing scream. As Stanley sat up he realized why: Doyle's bony skeletal arm had

ripped out of its socket and had held on
to him as he fell into
the boat. The
fingers were still
moving. Stanley
ripped it off his
shirt and threw it
into the water.

'Row, Daisy, row!'
he cried.

Inside, the grisly pair
snarled in despair, but their anger was over-
taken by the onset of the sickness. Beads of
black sweat began to form on their brows.

Stanley and Daisy did not speak on the
way back. They just kept rowing: at one
point Stanley swapped over with Daisy to
give her a rest, but he was all over the place
and Daisy was forced into doing it by herself.

In the distance, the ships of the Black Swarm veered to the north side of the island where they could sense the Ibis, resting in the ballast of the *Rusty Blade*.

The deadliest villains of the pirate world were about to collide.

'Are you all right, Daisy?' asked Stanley.

'Yeah, I'm fine,' she replied. 'Just fine. But tell me something. Did that go to plan or do I just not understand what's going on?'

'Don't worry. Like I said, it will work. The Ibis is on board the ship, but though she draws the pirates near she is protected.'

'By what?'

'Well, by the illness. Those villains are suffering, Daisy. They smelled awful, and they are on the brink of death. The power of the Ibis will speed up the sickness. All will be drawn to the ship, and all will die,' explained Stanley. It was a plan made in heaven. 'When they are all gone, we can return and retrieve the Ibis.'

Back on board the *Rusty Blade*, it was mayhem. Doyle and Seafood were fighting. Their knives were drawn and they danced around each other warily, stabbing the air.

'Stop this nonsense!' shouted Flanaghan. 'What's goin' on?'

'It's 'im,' cried Doyle. 'I lost me arm and he's laughin' at me!'

'How on earth did you manage that, Doyle? I only asked you two to see what the bloomin' noise was.'

And then something distracted Flanaghan. He turned and looked around, holding the lamp up inside the cabin. 'Something's different,' he began. 'I can feel it.'

'Feel what, sir?' asked Doyle.

'The Ibis. It's near. Somehow, closer than it was.' Flanaghan wanted to search, but the illness was becoming worse for all of them. Their skin grew more yellow and their fever boiled harder by the minute. It was only a matter of time before it had them firmly in its grip. They would take the Ibis first if they could, but they were all struggling.

'Tomorrow we will search hard,' Flanaghan claimed.

'But tonight I need rest.' He checked his reflection in a broken bottle and groaned at his weary expression. Then he took to his quarters and fell flat on his bed.

9

Scarecrow Point

Stanley and Daisy were struggling in the little
wooden boat, being blown around on the surf.
Up ahead an island loomed, and they were
sent crashing on to the rocks that spilled
around it.

'We'll have to stop here, Daisy. It's too
dangerous to go on.'

'No, not here,' insisted Daisy. 'That's

Scarecrow Point.'

'What's wrong with it?'
asked Stanley, frustrated.

'Stanley, Scarecrow
Point is haunted.'

'By what?' Stanley
grimaced doubtfully as she
pulled frantically on the oars,
gasping and wheezing.

'By a scarecrow. What else?' she
puffed. 'Once these hills were farmed,
but the story goes that a scarecrow came to
life and frightened the workers away. First the
scarecrow disappeared, then he was seen
waving his arms and screaming at passers-by.
No one comes here now.'

'Personally I have no faith in the
supernatural,' piped up a voice. It was the
pike, who had been listening all along.

'Daisy, I'm sorry. We have little choice,' cried Stanley, not caring for the tale of the scarecrow but caring more for his own life. 'And besides, you need the rest,' he insisted. They edged nearer to the rocky shore.

Finally they washed up on to the rocks and clambered out. Daisy held on tight to the pike and Stanley pulled the boat to safety in case it carried itself out to sea.

They struggled upward and found solace at the top of the Point, where the trees grew densely and there was good cover.

Stanley and Daisy watched the pirate ships grow nearer. It grew dark and cold but they were against the idea of lighting a campfire because it would only draw attention. They sat in fear and panic as the daylight faded fast. Despite Stanley's excellent plan, he felt he had no real way of knowing exactly what would happen.

Suddenly, Daisy saw a skinny muddy face with wild staring eyes appear behind Stanley. The little figure was dressed in rags with untamed hair and a matching beard.

Daisy screamed and Stanley would have done the same, but he was unable to catch his breath and wheezed pathetically.

'Children. At last. Where did you spring from? I have not seen anyone in years,' came the voice from the figure. It sounded surprisingly gentle, but that didn't stop Stanley and Daisy jumping to their feet and attempting to escape from the horrifying sight of the scarecrow come to life.

'Calm down, children. Calm down. I am a marooned islander from the Rock, abandoned here by pirates who attacked my boat. I do not intend to harm anyone. I only seek to leave this place.'

He was so frail and kind that they immediately believed him, and felt obliged to explain their own intentions.

'We are fleeing from the fleet of ships

heading this way,' stammered Stanley.

The straggly man got to his feet and stood staring out to sea at the pirate ships. 'In all my days I've never seen nothing like it,' he gasped. 'You really are in trouble. You need to keep moving. But don't go back to the Rock, not in the darkness. The curse of the wolf awaits you there.'

'You have been away a while, sir,' said Stanley. 'There is no longer any threat from the wolf.' He stared at the man they had thought was a scarecrow. 'But ... who are you? How do you know about the wolf?'

'Never mind me, son,' said the man. 'You can cross the island and continue from there. The water is safer on that side, and you're only a short journey from the Rock. I will help you move your boat and perhaps, on your return, you could get me help?'

They did as the strange man suggested. When Stanley and Daisy had climbed into the vessel, Stanley thanked him. 'Maybe it is better if you come with us,' suggested Stanley. 'Back to the island.'

The man looked at the boat. It was tiny. 'I think you have a full load already. I wouldn't wish to compromise your circumstances.'

'I do not wish to be rude,' began Stanley, 'but you are neither big nor heavy. I don't think you will make much difference.'

And as he spoke Daisy pushed up and patted the space beside her.

The man held his hands together. 'Thank you, children,' he said. 'I grow too old and weak to look after myself out here. It is cold and unwelcoming and at night it is as black as can be. Someday, I shall repay you.'

'Make yourself comfortable,' said Stanley.

'But you must tell us who you are.'

As the four of them set sail under the gathering moonlight, the pike fell gently to sleep and the man began his tale.

'I was a simple tradesman. But once whilst I was out fishing I was set upon by pirates, who wrecked my boat and left me stranded on that island, with only ploughed fields and an old scarecrow. I dismantled the scarecrow and took his clothes, then I learned to fend for myself. Often I would try to escape or catch the attention of passing ships, but all to no avail.'

As Stanley looked at him in the moonlight he saw how his straggly long-haired figure could have been mistaken for the shape of some mad scarecrow spirit, dancing around with desperate flailing arms.

'And what name do you go by?' asked Stanley.

'My name is Victor. Victor Carelli. And I
hope that somewhere, my wife still waits
for me.'

Stanley and Daisy stared at each other in
wild surprise. But they did not say anything.
Not yet.

The Missing Link

The boat bobbed along on the water and
soon they were soon close to the island.
They hit land and began to walk across
the moor.

Victor felt good being back on the Rock.
He could see the twinkle of candlelight down
in the houses, and a flutter of excitement
leaped around inside him.

As they hit the gypsy camp, Bartley appeared through the darkness.

'Come to the tents!' he shouted.

The travellers greeted Victor with open arms. Even here, he had many old friends. They had known of his disappearance and now they rejoiced at his return. Someone wrapped a blanket round him and sat him by the fire. Someone else brought him a hot broth and everyone gathered round, staring at his wild appearance in astonishment touched with amusement.

But inside the main tent, Greta was warning the children and readying them for surprise.

'Prepare yourself, Stanley. They draw near, but we are right behind you. In the meantime there is something further. I know you keep secrets well, but do you have room in your heart for another?'

Stanley wore an expression of confusion. 'I suppose so,' he said, not knowing what was coming next but feeling that it might be something important.

'And you, Daisy. Can you be faithful to your friend here and protect a lamb from the prying eyes of wolves?' Greta asked.

'Of course,' said Daisy firmly, equally perplexed.

'Then pull back the velvet fringe that runs around the bottom of the table, my dear, and tell me what you see,' Greta requested.

Daisy did as she was asked, and before their eyes lay the beautifully crafted shape of the silver casket. Lost for thousands of years, and only seen by few. It took Stanley's breath away and he felt a rush of blood to the head. He was looking at something he thought he would not see in his lifetime.

'Now you know why the gypsies came, Stanley,' murmured Greta. 'We came to thank you for what you gave to us. The freedom to return to Crampton Rock. What you see before you is yours,' explained Greta gently. She urged them to look more closely at it.

The casket looked perfect, forged so beautifully and intricately in shining silver that seemed to echo every other colour when the light was on it, just like the Ibis.

Its shape was rectangular and the lid rounded like an old pirate's chest. It had little short legs and they too were intricately formed. Every bit of it was unique. It was only small, though. Smaller than Stanley had expected.

But when they examined it in detail, they could see that something was missing.

Stanley looked at the sections of the lock. It was just as Admiral Swift had described it: a Jackal and a Bison, and then a space where the missing Ibis fitted.

At first he did not dare touch the casket, but then he could not resist. It was heavy. Perhaps something inside was making it so.

But he would not know what that was until he placed the Ibis in the lock and opened the lid.

'It has carried many secrets over the years, Stanley. What she hides now, I cannot say. Something important, I am sure,' said Greta. 'Take it home, and when the time is right you can open it there.'

'You must reveal its contents in secrecy,' said Bartley, who was standing by Stanley. 'It is yours now, and a private matter between you and the casket.'

They went home across the moor in wild excitement. Bartley escorted them as far as the long path that led to the house, and waited until they were safely inside.

In a flash, before anything else was dealt with, the casket was out of sight in Stanley's room. It would have to lie in hiding there until, he hoped, he would again get his hands on the Ibis. The pike was stowed away back in his cupboard.

Finally, the boat crew sat Victor in the kitchen, preparing him to meet the house-keeper of Candlestick Hall.

'Listen, Victor,' began Daisy. 'There is a lady who works here, and she will be interested to see you. She will arrive shortly, and will probably be looking for us, and will be angry, I'm sure – but I feel you may change her mood.'

Mrs Carelli burst through the door. She had been out, desperately searching for Stanley and Daisy.

'Stanley Buggles, where have you b—? Who is thi—?'

Victor stood up. He looked wearily at the woman he had married, and who he'd thought he would never see again.

'Violet … it's me,' he said, and his eyes filled up uncontrollably. 'I'm back.' His voice wobbled and tears left clean streaks across his muddy face. 'Oh Victor, my goodness.' Mrs Carelli held her hands up to her mouth, and for a second she looked like she was about to drop to the floor. But then she ran forward and grabbed him close in her arms.

His tiny figure bent like a rag doll as she held on to him tight.

'Is this the bit where we disappear?' suggested Daisy.

'Ahh … yes,' agreed Stanley, and they slipped out of the way.

They headed upstairs to stare at the casket again, and went to the window to look upon the boats.

It looked like Stanley's plan was working. The endless fleet was heading north, to the small bay where the *Rusty Blade* drew them near.

Stanley turned to Daisy. They shook hands and grinned happily.

Shortly after, Victor
was sitting on a tall
stool in the kitchen,
and Daisy was
making use of her
hairdressing skills to
tidy him up.

Mrs Carelli looked
on in admiration as
clumps of hair fell to
the floor and she saw
the face of the man
she knew reappear
before her.

His face was
drawn and thin and
he had what Stanley's
mother called a
weather tan.

(It was the way she described the look of someone who worked outside.)

Then the beard began to come off and Victor felt at his smooth face. It had been years since he had run his hands across his chin. Mrs Carelli began to cry when she saw his face.

'Oh Violet, please!' said Victor. 'Don't start me off again!'

'I still can't believe it,' she wept. 'I had this awful feeling that when we shaved your hair off we'd find out it was somebody else under there. But it's really you,' she blubbered.

And they all laughed. It was a nice moment and Stanley forgot his troubles as he and Daisy helped to comfort Mrs Carelli.

But he knew there was work to do and that they should really be readying themselves for … well, for anything.

The best place for them to be was out on the moor and the best company for them to be in was with the travellers.

Stanley and Daisy left Mr and
Mrs Carelli at the house and
headed for the hills.

11

The Coming of the Angel

There was to be no sleep that night on board the *Rusty Blade*. Nor would there be on any other pirate vessel. The ships were heading frantically now towards the north side of the island where the *Rusty Blade* was lying, its Yellow Jack now missing. And no one that rushed towards it knew that on board a deadly disease awaited. As the Ibis lay sleepily in its hiding place, its presence made the fever boil.

Stanley and Daisy were now making toward the gypsy camp, where Greta sat waiting for them. She had seen them coming through the crystal ball.

The campfire glowed in the darkness and they scrambled across the moor towards the orange light.

Bartley came to meet them. 'It is good to see you both. You are most welcome,' he greeted them. 'We are readying ourselves in case we are needed.'

Stanley saw that the travellers were making weapons, practising the art of swordsmanship and close combat. He felt warmed by it.

'Quickly, now. Come and see what is happening,' beckoned Greta.

She ran her hands over her crystal ball and looked hard through the whirling white mist.

'Look how they fight among themselves,' she grinned. Stanley and Daisy could see nothing in the glass ball, but waited on Greta's every word.

'All the ships are closing in on the *Rusty Blade*. The Ibis draws them near. As they close in, the pirates are growing desperate to reach the Ibis. Not only are the ships attacking those around them, the shipmates also turn on each other. This is indeed a plan made in heaven, children, and I watched you put it into place. Well done. You are braver than most,' Greta said warmly.

'I couldn't have done it if you hadn't explained the purpose of the Yellow Jack,' smiled Stanley.

Drinks arrived, and they sat in comfort for

a while. Finally, Stanley and Daisy decided that they must return to the Hall to sleep out the night.

The sea bed changed beneath the feet of Angel Cuzco. It went from fine white sand to rocks here and there, and then suddenly it was nothing but pebbles and fine shale. Up ahead the water grew shallow, and eventually the golden-white mane of hair that hung from his skull showed itself on the surface.

Next his emerald-green eyes stared out from the shallow surf, and he kept on marching at the same pace until his soaking-wet skeletal form had emerged fully from the ocean waves.

After Stanley and Daisy had left, Greta saw something appear in the glass ball that would have forced her to keep the children in the camp.

The deathly figure of Angel Cuzco was walking across the harbour of Crampton Rock, heading for the moor. His emerald eyes grew greener as he felt the Ibis so strongly he would have sworn it beat like a heart inside him.

His passion for the Ibis turned into anger as he drew closer. If anything stood in his way, he would tear it to pieces.

Greta called for Bartley and Phinn to guard the children. The Angel was coming their way, but the best thing they could do was to let him head for the *Rusty Blade*.

Stanley and Daisy were still making their way across the moor, unaware. Up ahead, two small green lights were approaching across the plain. Stanley thought of all sorts of things it could be. A werewolf. The pirates. It could be anything … but as they drew nearer they saw a scarlet-coated, white-haired shape descending on them.

Bartley was running up behind. 'Stop!' he cried.

It was too late. Angel Cuzco was right before them.

But the children were nothing to him and he never even took a glance. They didn't come into his plan, and he simply walked right through them. As he did so a force knocked them to the floor, leaving them breathless.

Bartley and Phinn showed their battle-worn hands and prepared for the scarlet phantom. The Angel swiped at Bartley with his sword, and using the elbow of the same arm he forced a blow under Phinn's chin. Phinn dropped to the floor but stood straight back up again. He was made of iron. Bartley placed a hard right hand into Cuzco's ribs and they smashed into pieces.

But the spirit had an advantage: he felt no pain.

Stanley and Daisy by now had got to their feet and they joined in. Daisy jumped on the Angel's back and yanked on his hair. Stanley was throwing a tirade of punches but none of them was landing.

Then Cuzco dropped his sword and, using both hands and a supernatural speed, he somehow grabbed Phinn and Bartley by the hair and pulled their heads together. *Crack.* They fell to the ground.

Cuzco picked up his blade and tucked it into his belt. Then he turned to Stanley and Daisy.

'When I return from the ships I will hang you urchins from the gallows,' he promised. The Angel grinned a sickly smile and marched towards the north bay. Greta's glass ball clouded over. The whirling mist became a green fog and she could see nothing.

The gypsy encampment was in a frenzy.
They headed to the bay, not knowing what
they would find.

12

the North Bay Battle

The *Rusty Blade* was surrounded. You could not have counted the number of black silhouettes of sails and flags that swayed in the fresh gust, whirling in circles around the bay. Screaming and shouting filled the air. As the ships neared each other, cannonballs began hurtling through the darkness and clouds of gunpowder popped here and there in the night.

'Drive my ancient spirit unto the sacred bird. Deliver thy casket forged of silver. Prepare for the coming of the Angel, for he walks alone among the dead,'

recited Cuzco to himself. He watched from
the clifftop as the fleet descended on the
Rusty Blade, sitting helplessly in the middle of
the mayhem.

Some pirates jumped from their ships into
the water and climbed up the sides. Others
clambered across the rigging of their own
ships and jumped down on to the deck.
Many sat back and simply fired everything
they had at everybody else.

But on board the *Rusty Blade*, no one made

any effort to defend the ship. No one moved
at all.

Scribbles Flanaghan, one of the
deadliest pirates ever to sail the salty waters,
lay face down on the floor with his last ever
drink of grog held loosely in his palm. Young
Master Phipps had retired to his bed, never
to make it out of his bedclothes again.

Seafood Smith was slumped over a table with a plate of tentacles and seaweed sauce spilled down his shirt. And Doyle the Dentist, whose torturous treatment was the scourge of the seven seas, lay on his back with his best pair of pliers by his side.

Every one of the gruesome crew was dead from the buccaneer's bones, with yellow skin and slimy boils about their bodies. Their green tongues hung out like slabs of rancid meat and their eyeballs had turned black.

And now, just as the crafty mind of Stanley Buggles had planned, the rest of the pirate fraternity climbed on board – unknowingly to embrace the deadly infection that now burned at a thundering pace.

Out on the upper deck, the clash of phantom pirate enemies had begun. They swung awkwardly at each other with cudgels and blades and cursed each other's names.

Two rogues battled tirelessly. Another appeared and jumped in to help a hook-handed friend. Suddenly, all three of them were pounced upon by an unknown who swung with a shining cutlass at everything in front of him. But the dispute was settled by a cannonball that sang through the air and bowled them effortlessly apart.

Muddy, blackened faces appeared over the side, their owners ambling unnoticed into the bowels of the ship to begin their search. But there were others in the darkness, and a blind fight ensued among the sickly searchers.

Very quickly their bodies became listless
and weary. They were drawn to the Ibis,
every one, but as they came they were caught

in Stanley's effortless trap. The fever boiled on their brows and the energy of the ancient Ibis spiralled it into a furious force.

There were hundreds of pirates, but soon their grubby corpses lay scattered across the decks. Some had died from the fever and some from the battle but still more came.

Angel Cuzco appeared as if from nowhere. His long white hair and scarlet coat glowed in the darkness, and the lights of his emerald-green eyes were enough to frighten the fiercest of men. But still he was forced into savage battle.

Stanley and Daisy had joined back up with the gypsies and now the full force of the Crampton army stood in silhouette along the clifftop. They watched the North Bay Battle from the safety of the hills.

Through the stinking, filthy, fly-blown
darkness the pirates battled and searched for
the treasure all night.

But soon every pirate was either dead or burning with the fever.

After hours of vicious pandemonium the pirates who were left grew distracted from the fight, drawn by the Ibis.

Still they sweated at the brow and felt the slimy boils pop up on their skin. They did not notice the illness that grew upon them. They found themselves almost hypnotized by the Ibis, as each and every one of them searched among the stones that lined the bottom of the *Rusty Blade*.

All except for Angel Cuzco, who stood staring hard at the pebbles, almost as if he could see right through them and then when he found the spot he would walk right over to it.

And that's exactly what he did.

He was strong, stronger than most. He did not feel a fever or a shaking in his limbs. No. It would take more than that, he had told himself.

Stomping his way through the crowd of sickly pirates, he sank his hand deep down to where Stanley had laid the Ibis. He wrapped his bony joints around her and plucked her from her nest.

Then, without a moment's thought, he stood up straight and climbed to the upper deck. The pirates that still littered the ship were on their knees. The fever was taking their lives quickly and as they lay upon the deck their gruesome features rotted and left their stinking bones behind.

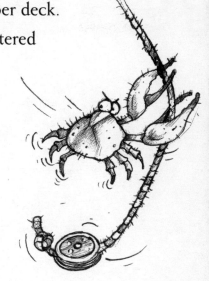

It grew quieter and quieter as the noise of gunfire and the screams of war were replaced by the silent grip of death.

The ships lay battered and broken on the rocks, and soon the evidence of their stay would be swallowed up by the gulf.

The Pirate Wolves

But Angel Cuzco was not done. He did not seem affected by the germs that had been the buccaneers' downfall. He was strong and he was hungry, and he had not come this far only to suffer illness.

He walked around the deck in the early morning light, picking his way through the bones and keeping the heads of those he knew belonged to the hardest of pirate captains, holding them by their hair: those he had fought in the past and those he had struggled to beat that very night.

With his arms full and his sword tucked by his side, Angel Cuzco headed for the gypsy encampment.

'Put the children in the wagons!' someone cried out.

Suddenly the travellers were preparing for the onslaught. Weapons appeared and the horses were brought forward. Bartley and Phinn were stripped to the waist, their fists held high.

A huge crowd of troops stood in wait: some on horseback, some on foot, many with weapons and many armed with hardened fists that knew their trade.

The crazy stare of Angel Cuzco came

close. Now he wanted the silver casket, and he wanted it desperately. The gypsies could see that he was alone, but that he carried something in his hands.

Inside her tent, Greta had been looking into her ball and she cried out in panic when she saw familiar eyes peering back at her.

'Wolves!' she cried. 'I thought we were free of the wolves. Why do they show themselves in the glass?'

Before she could see clear, the green mist came again and choked the picture in the ball.

And outside Angel Cuzco stood before the crowd.

The travellers' army looked strong. They would be a handful even for the Angel, and especially since he stood alone.

But something was about to happen.

Angel Cuzco scattered the skulls around him, then began to whisper his words once more.

'Deliver thy casket forged of silver. Prepare for the coming of the Angel, for he walks alone among the dead.'

He took his sword and split each skull down its middle. From each shattered head emerged a black shape.

At first it was not clear what had materialized, but after only moments, a huge pack of wolves stood by the side of Angel Cuzco. Grisly, slavering, hungry, filthy wolves.

If there was a sure way to frighten the travellers, it was the sight of the wolves. They had already suffered too much at the mercy of these animals.

But bravery welled up inside them and they stood together.

Bartley took a long look. Before him were the beasts that had taken his brother. His fear never surfaced: the feeling of anger pushed it deep back down into his stomach, and he stood tall at the front of his army.

Suddenly it began. The beasts lurched
forward and darted speedily in the direction
of their enemy, and the travellers fought back
with fists and cudgels. The horses circled
and pushed the wolves back,
but they bit awkwardly at
their heels and the first
blood was drawn.
Cuzco danced
around with his arms
whipping up
a storm as he
slashed his
blade through
the air. Bartley
and Phinn held
him off with
poles of wood and
shields made from

152

barrel tops. But the wolves snaked in around anyone who came close and snapped at them: it was impossible. The dogs reacted, barking with bared teeth, but they were anxious against the might of the black wolves.

As the mist settled again in Greta's ball something else came clear. Faces. Evil, yellow-eyed faces with shining blades held fast between their rotting teeth. Where did they come from?

Latecomers! The very last of the ghostly pirate ships. Three of them, all filled with sea scoundrels of one kind and another and all of them avoiding the fever of the *Rusty Blade*.

Instead, they were heading for the excitement out on the moor, where they grasped a vague sniff of the Ibis. They scrabbled their way on to the cliffs over rocks and boulders.

It was Daisy who noticed them first. She hurled rocks at them and forced them back, but somehow they made it through and now the Crampton army was surrounded.

Whether Daisy and Stanley liked it or not, they were in the middle of the fight. Every so often someone would pull them back and push them to one side, but they were not the kind to stand and watch and it was not the first time they had been eye to eye with the full force of the supernatural.

Cuzco moved so fast it was hard to see him. His long white hair flew about his head as he turned and twisted, thrusting wounds here and there.

There were several travellers injured by
now but they pushed on bravely. Stanley
became worried that the spirit of Cuzco
could not be defeated no matter what.

The screams and shouts of battle were
raised. The crunch of clogs on bones, the
thwack of poles and sticks, the whoosh and
swipe of the blade and the cries and screams
of pure pain.

Stanley remembered all the moves that
Bartley had shown him: throwing punches
then moving swiftly out of danger, staying
on his toes so he could nimbly step back
or forward. Daisy had watched him often,
and she followed his lead. They plagued
the new arrivals with fast moves, and when
they had them confused and distracted
the dogs moved in and took chunks out of
their legs.

These pirates were not affected by the illness, but still they were foul and rancid as they came up close.

Stanley was pounced upon. Three skeletal fiends pinned him to the floor. A fourth approached with something heavy and he was about to bring it down on the boy.

Thud. Good old Daisy.

Armed with a pole, she had brought the villain to the ground and now she ran at the rest with it held out lengthways. Three bony buccaneers fell like skittles, shattering into pieces.

But from their fragments they reassembled, and the impossible task continued.

The clash and clang of metal and the force of whacks and blows prevailed over the moor. Only the howls of dogs and wolves could drown them.

The Angel tore through the crowd, leaving many injured. But it was the good fortune of Crampton Rock that he saw every man as his enemy, and soon he tore into the last of the pirates. They sensed that he had the ancient prize, and every one of them was drawn to him, but he cut into them so fast his triumph was effortless.

Then, in what to Stanley seemed like slow motion, there was a moment of suffering on the face of the Angel. Sweat was pouring from his brow, and it appeared as if his supernatural force was waning.

Perhaps he had given all the fight he had. Maybe his efforts had sapped all his energy.

But no, it was not the fight that tired him, it was the fever. And now his sweat was black.

He had fought so hard all night and all day he had not stopped to notice that he too was ailing. His blade grew slower, his movements more shallow.

The tide had turned and now the gypsy blows came thick and fast. The wolves grew slower too, panting and heaving, losing their appetite for blood.

In a final attempt to win the battle, Angel Cuzco raised his sword up high to deal a fatal swipe to Stanley.

But the mighty Bartley sent a crushing blow into the Angel's middle and his bony carcass shattered into pieces and scattered over the ground.

And as it did so the wolves fell too.

Angel Cuzco's broad cutlass dropped,

the point of its blade landing perilously close
to Stanley who by now had fallen to the
floor. It pinned the collar of his shirt to the
ground, and he was so shaken that he fainted
there and then.

He came round to the feel of a tongue
lashing across his face. It was one of the
gypsy dogs, desperate to bring him back. He
stroked her face and laughed, then jumped to
his feet.

The enemy lay defeated on the ground
and the whole of the gypsy encampment
roared in triumph.

Stanley took a close look at his enemy.
The light from the two emerald eyes was
dying out like failing candles, turning to
sheer black. His body and those of all the
wolves turned from grisly mangy festering

skin to pure white bone in moments. And before long every scrap of proof that they had ever even been had wisped into the air, and the only thing left was the shining silver amulet that they all knew to be the Ibis.

Stanley grasped it tightly and tucked it away in his pocket.

'Come and speak to Greta,' said Phinn.

Stanley and Daisy followed him back to Greta's tent amongst cheers and roars. There would be celebration soon, but they would need some sleep first. Stanley had been away from home for too long and he knew the consequences, but right now he was not too concerned. His biggest worries had been dealt with.

'Come in, Stanley, Daisy,' said Greta. 'Take a drink, and a moment to calm yourselves down.'

They sat and talked a while, and soon they were laughing and joking. 'Go on, Stanley,' smiled Greta. 'Take yourself off now – after all, you'll have some explaining to do when you get back. And we'll be happy for you to pay us a visit whenever you please. You too, Daisy.'

So much had happened, yet Stanley and Daisy barely spoke on the way back, either through shock or tiredness or a combination of both. They stopped every now and then and stared at the peaceful harbour. They would soon be back to reality.

They made their entry to the house

through the old fuel store, hoping to sneak in unnoticed and pretend they had been around for longer than they had.

In theory it was a good plan, but when they'd climbed in they could hear the adults in the kitchen. It was twice as hard to avoid detection now Violet had Victor back.

Stanley and Daisy could hear the Carellis in full discussion about their whereabouts. And then, a stroke of luck: it sounded like they were putting on their coats and heading out to find them.

Good. Time to move through the house.

In they sneaked, like bilge rats slinking over the ballast of the ship, lurking and snooping, then darting through the winding corridors until they arrived safely in the comfort of Stanley's room.

With bated breath, they placed the silver casket on the chest under the window. Stanley fumbled in his pocket for the cloth-covered Ibis. She did not bear any scars, despite her long journey since she left the comfort of the pike's belly.

Stanley flicked out the two prongs at the back of the Ibis. His great-uncle, Admiral Swift, had explained this part to him, though he had thought he would never see the day when the Ibis and the casket were reunited. Then Stanley lined her up with the empty space in the lock. He gently pushed it inward and waited until a neat *click* sounded.

Daisy looked at Stanley and Stanley looked at Daisy. He turned the small horizontal bar until it was in a vertical position and it clicked again.

Stanley felt the lid release its age-old

grip, and they peered inside.

'*Candles?*' they both asked.

Stanley counted them. '… Four, five, six candles. Mmmmm.'

He and Daisy took them out and stared at them for a good while. There was nothing special about them, or at least it didn't seem as though there was. After all, it was only wax. No sign or special mark about them except for a small 'C' stamped in the base of each one.

The casket alone was enough to set their hearts alight, but the candles were a mystery.

'Perhaps there was nothing in particular inside it, so someone thought it was a good place to store things?' suggested Daisy.

'Maybe,' said Stanley. It didn't matter.

Later, he found the perfect place for the silver casket behind the false panel in his cupboard, and it was safely out of sight. After all, he did not know when sinister company would next throw a shadow across his door.

Beyond the Candlelight

The children were foolish to think they could avoid the adults for ever and that night Stanley had to endure a dreadful argument. He was in serious trouble, confined to his room.

Disappearing for days at a time! Nowhere to be seen! No messages left! Nothing! Mrs Carelli couldn't cope with it. It would have to stop.

Daisy was sent home and suffered equally when she returned to her aunt and uncle.

Stanley knew he would have to weather the storm and wait until Mrs Carelli's anger had blown over.

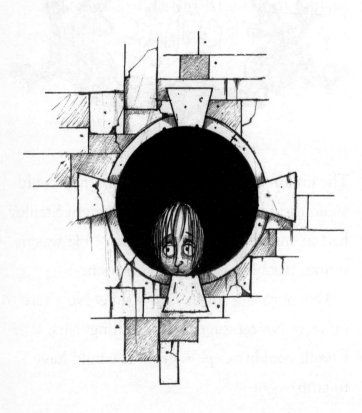

He spent hours looking over the intricacies of the silver casket. However closely he looked, there was always something new to see. Strange patterns and shapes; little heads of lions; the claws and tails of slinking lizards, each of them like a tiny silver gargoyle, winding their way around the casket almost as if they were alive.

He saw his confinement to the house as a way of closely watching over this ancient treasure. There were always adventures to be had inside. He could live there for ever and still find a new doorway the next day. And there was always the bronze warrior if he felt brave enough to sneak out for a while.

It was a perfect day. The sun broke across the harbour, and the tide was right back. For once Crampton Rock really was peaceful.

Victor had taken up his new role in the house marvellously. He was out pruning the trees and clipping the lawn edgings while Mrs Carelli was busy creating something in the kitchen.

'It's a nice day!' said Stanley, with his eyes glaring expectantly at Mrs Carelli.

'Go on then,' she said, giving in. 'You can go out. Just as long as you don't disappear.'

'Of course I won't,' he answered. He decided he would take a little time to help Victor, and maybe get to know him better. Picking up some pruning shears, he began to make a mess of something.

'Here, son,' came Victor's voice. 'Like this.' In his gentle way he took the time to show Stanley what to do, and soon they were like old friends, chatting away and working together.

Mrs Carelli looked out of the kitchen window. It was years since she had watched Victor as he tidied the rose beds or raked the grass, in their own little garden back in the village. His hair had turned to white in the time he had been missing and he was much thinner than he'd ever been.

She shrugged off a single tear and went back to her work with a smile.

Stanley and Victor were locked in conversation.

'Have you always lived here?' Stanley questioned.

'My family have been here for years. My father, my father's father and his father before him. All of us continued the business in the village, one after the other.'

'Were you fishermen?'

'Oh no, son. We were candle makers.

The old shop still sits in the village, but the door has not been opened since I left the island all those years ago. Violet could not bring herself to go there while I was gone, so she took the job as housekeeper for  Admiral Swift. Perhaps I will return there some day soon.'

'I see. And do you mind if I ask you about the pirates who attacked you?' asked Stanley.

'Well, I guess I don't mind. I haven't really talked about it too much.'

Stanley detected a sadness in his tone.

'Perhaps we should talk of something else,' he suggested. He had no intention of upsetting poor Victor.

'Not at all,' said Victor. 'It'll do me good to speak of it. I should not harbour the memory all to myself.'

And he began.

'I'd set out one afternoon when the tide had lifted the boats in the harbour, intending to go fishing. I had candles for a small island that sits north-west of here and I thought I would see what I could catch on the way. I had only reached the west coast of Crampton Rock, just short of Scarecrow Point, when they appeared.

'A real band of rogues they were. Their own vessel was bigger than mine, much bigger, and they saw that I was alone. I was an easy target. They approached me and when they found out what I was carrying they came aboard and took my stock.

'They abandoned me on the island and cannonballed my boat to smithereens.'

'I don't understand,' said Stanley. 'Why would pirates be interested in your *candles?*'

'Good question, Stanley, but there is sound reasoning behind it. Believe it or not, candle trading is dangerous business where pirates dwell.'

'Why on earth is that?' quizzed Stanley.

'Well, when piracy was rife in these parts and treasures of one kind and another were passed from rogue to rogue and buried here and there, maps were hidden in all sorts of places.

'Many years ago, pirates knocked on the door of my father's shop at the dead of night. At gunpoint they forced him to make six

candles. Each one concealed a rolled-up
section of a large map.

'When they left they were savaged by the
werewolf as they escaped across the moor,
and the candles disappeared. They were
never found. I can only guess where they
are now.

'The pirates from their crew did not
believe in the werewolf, and we were blamed
by them for the murders and for stealing
the map. It made life hard for us. Eventually
the mystery of the Carelli candles became
notorious, and many came in search of them.
Your Great-Uncle Bart was one of them,
Stanley, and although he was never to find
them, he gave up his pirate life and bought
Darkling Hall, renaming it Candlestick Hall
after his long search for the Carelli candles.'

Stanley stood with eyes wide open.

'I promised you that one day I would repay
you for your kindness. I hope that what I
have told you is of help,' Victor said, with a
knowing look.

'Oh, it is, Victor. It really is.' Stanley
smiled at him, then he cleared away his tools
and set off back into the house.

There was something he had to do.

Scribbles from the

Something Wickedly Weird

sketchbook.

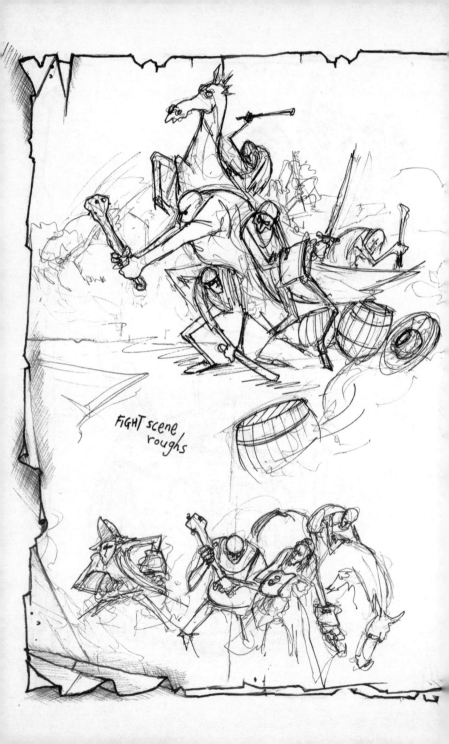

FIGHT scene roughs

Pirate Ship's Cat.

Chris Mould

Chris Mould went to art school at the age of sixteen. During this time, he did various jobs, from delivering papers to washing-up and cooking in a kitchen. He has won the Nottingham Children's Book Award and been commended for the Sheffield. He loves his work and likes to write and draw the kind of books that he would have liked to have on his shelf as a boy. He is married with two children and lives in Yorkshire.

Crampton Rock seems the perfect place to spend a long summer holiday. But there's always something to go and spoil it all, isn't there?

Why are all the **dogs three-legged**? Is there really a **werewolf** on the loose? And what do the *pirates* want with Stanley Buggles...?

S♦METHING
WICKEDLY
WEIRD

The Werewolf and the Ibis

CHRIS MOULD

All looks crisp and cosy in
Crampton Rock as Stanley Buggles
settles down for the winter.
But something wicked has blown
in with the wind.

What is the **headless ghost**
of Admiral Swift desperate to tell Stanley?

And who are the *deadly pirates*,
marching through the oncoming blizzard ...?

SOMETHING
WICKEDLY
WEIRD

The Ice Pirates

CHRIS MOULD

The island of **Crampton Rock** has emerged from **pirate battle**. But something far more sinister is on the move...

What claim does the **Darkling family** have on Stanley Buggles' home?

And do the Darkling twins really keep a **two-headed snake** as a pet?

S**O**METHING
WICKEDLY
WEIRD
The Curse of the Wolf

CHRIS MOULD

Stanley Buggles holds the key
to the **smugglers' map**.

But does he **dare** to uncover
its **ancient secrets**?

What will happen if he ventures down
into the **treacherous tunnels?**

And who is *following* behind ...?

SOMETHING
WICKEDLY
WEIRD
The Smugglers' Secret

CHRIS MOULD

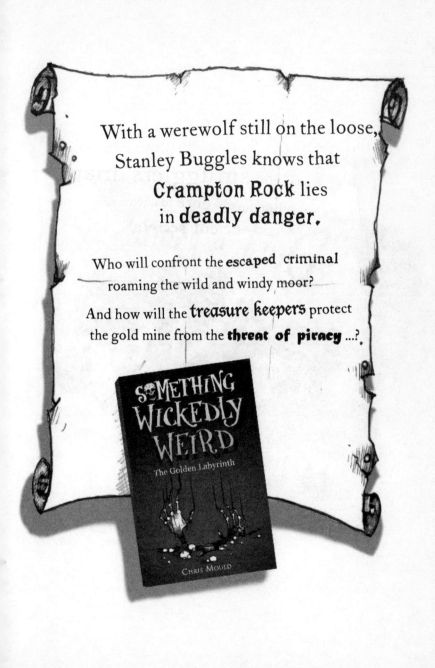

With a werewolf still on the loose,
Stanley Buggles knows that
Crampton Rock lies
in **deadly danger.**

Who will confront the **escaped** criminal
roaming the wild and windy moor?
And how will the **treasure keepers** protect
the gold mine from the **threat of piracy** ...?

SOMETHING
WICKEDLY
WEIRD
The Golden Labyrinth

CHRIS MOULD

Are you prepared to be scared?

This book contains ten of the most
terrifying tales, adapted, written and
superbly illustrated by award-winner

Chris Mould

Five are original ghost stories, and five
are retellings of classic tales,
from *The Legend of Sleepy Hollow*
by Washington Irving to *The Tell-Tale Heart*
by Edgar Allen Poe.

Open this book at your own peril ...